What Kids Say About
Carole Marsh Mysteries . . .

"I love the real locations! Reading the book always makes me want to go and visit them all on our next family vacation. My Mom says maybe, but I can't wait!"

"One day, I want to be a real kid in one of Ms. Marsh's mystery books. I think it would be fun, and I think I am a real character anyway. I filled out the application and sent it in and am keeping my fingers crossed!"

"History was not my favorite subject till I starting reading Carole Marsh Mysteries. Ms. Marsh really brings history to life. Also, she leaves room for the scary and fun."

"I think Christina is so smart and brave. She is lucky to be in the mystery books because she gets to go to a lot of places. I always wonder just how much of the book is true and what is made up. Trying to figure that out is fun!"

"Grant is cool and funny! He makes me laugh a lot!!"

"I like that there are boys and girls in the story of different ages. Some mysteries I outgrow, but I can always find a favorite character to identify with in these books."

"They are scary, but not too scary. They are funny. I learn a lot. There is always food which makes me hungry. I feel like I am there."

What Parents and Teachers Say About Carole Marsh Mysteries . . .

"I think kids love these books because they have such a wealth of detail. I know I learn a lot reading them! It's an engaging way to look at the history of any place or event. I always say I'm only going to read one chapter to the kids, but that never happens–it's always two or three, at least!"
–Librarian

"Reading the mystery and going on the field trip–Scavenger Hunt in hand–was the most fun our class ever had! It really brought the place and its history to life. They loved the real kids characters and all the humor. I loved seeing them learn that reading is an experience to enjoy!"
–4th grade teacher

"Carole Marsh is really on to something with these unique mysteries. They are so clever; kids want to read them all. The Teacher's Guides are chock full of activities, recipes, and additional fascinating information. My kids thought I was an expert on the subject–and with this tool, I felt like it!"
–3rd grade teacher

"My students loved writing their own Real Kids/Real Places mystery book! Ms. Marsh's reproducible guidelines are a real jewel. They learned about copyright and more & ended up with their own book they were so proud of!"
–Reading/Writing Teacher

"The kids seem very realistic–my children seemed to relate to the characters. Also, it is educational by expanding their knowledge about the famous places in the books."

"They are what children like: mysteries and adventures with children they can relate to."

"Encourages reading for pleasure."

"This series is great. It can be used for reluctant readers, and as a history supplement."

CAROLE MARSH MYSTERIES™

The Rip-ROARING
Mystery on the

African
Safari

South Africa

by Carole Marsh

Carole Marsh Mysteries™ and its skull colophon are the property of
Carole Marsh and Gallopade International.

Published by Gallopade International/Carole Marsh Books. Printed in the
United States of America.

Managing Editor: Sherry Moss
Senior Editor: Janice Baker
Assistant Editor: Michael Kelly
Cover Design: Yvonne Ford
Cover Photo Credits: istock.com, clipart.com, photos.com
Content Design and Illustrations: Yvonne Ford

Gallopade International is introducing SAT words that kids need to
know in each new book we publish. The SAT words are bold in the
story. Look for this special logo beside each word in the glossary.
Happy Learning!

Gallopade is proud to be a member and supporter of these educational
organizations and associations:

American Booksellers Association
American Library Association
International Reading Association
National Association for Gifted Children
The National School Supply and Equipment Association
The National Council for the Social Studies
Museum Store Association
Association of Partners for Public Lands
Association of Booksellers for Children
Association for the Study of African American Life and History
National Alliance of Black School Educators

30 Years Ago . . .

As a mother and an author, one of the fondest periods of my life was when I decided to write mystery books for children. At this time (1979) kids were pretty much glued to the TV, something parents and teachers complained about the way they do about web surfing and blogging today.

I decided to set each mystery in a real place—a place kids could go and visit for themselves after reading the book. And I also used real children as characters. Usually a couple of my own children served as characters, and I had no trouble recruiting kids from the book's location to also be characters.

Also, I wanted all the kids—boys and girls of all ages—to participate in solving the mystery. And, I wanted kids to learn something as they read. Something about the history of the location. And I wanted the stories to be funny. That formula of real+scary+smart+fun served me well.

I love getting letters from teachers and parents who say they read the book with their class or child, then visited the historic site and saw all the places in the mystery for themselves. What's so great about that? What's great is that you and your children have an experience that bonds you together forever. Something you shared. Something you both cared about at the time. Something that crossed all age levels—a good story, a good scare, a good laugh!

30 years later,

Carole Marsh

Hey, kids! As you see—here we are ready to embark on another of our exciting Carole Marsh Mystery adventures! You know, in "real life," I keep very close tabs on Christina, Grant, and their friends when we travel. However, in the mystery books, they always seem to slip away from Papa and me so that they can try to solve the mystery on their own!

I hope you will go to www.carolemarshmysteries.com and apply to be a character in a future mystery book! Well, the *Mystery Girl* is all tuned up and ready for "take-off!"

Gotta go...Papa says so! Wonder what I've forgotten this time?

Happy "Armchair Travel" Reading,

Mimi

About the Characters

 **Christina**, age 10: Mysterious things really do happen to her! Hobbies: soccer, Girl Scouts, anything crafty, hanging out with Mimi, and going on new adventures.

 **Grant**, age 7: Always manages to fall off boats, back into cactuses, and find strange clues—even in real life! Hobbies: camping, baseball, computer games, math, and hanging out with Papa.

 **Mimi** is Carole Marsh, children's book author and creator of Carole Marsh Mysteries, Around the World in 80 Mysteries, Three Amigos Mysteries, Baby's First Mysteries, and many others.

 **Papa** is Bob Longmeyer, the author's real-life husband, who really does wear a tuxedo, cowboy boots and hat, fly an airplane, captain a boat, speak in a booming voice, and laugh a lot!

Travel around the world with Christina and Grant as they visit famous places in 80 countries, and experience the mysterious happenings that always seem to follow them!

Books in This Series

Table of Contents

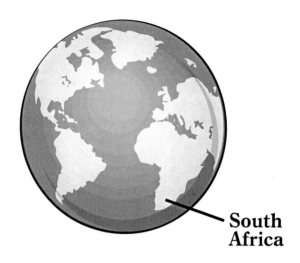

South
Africa

Algeria

Nigeria

Ethiopia

ATLANTIC
OCEAN

Johannesburg
x

Madagascar

HURRY UP AND WAIT

Grant woke from the jolt when the aircraft touched down on the long runway. He rubbed his eyes and glanced out the tiny window. Scenery rolled past at a decreasing rate as the aircraft slowed on its way to the terminal.

We're in Johannesburg, South Africa, Grant thought to himself, as the aircraft turned off the runway. He knew this was going to be a great trip. He could feel it in his bones. The aircraft passed several maintenance hangers, which had a few aircraft in various stages of repair outside on their ramps. Aircraft technicians climbed over them like worker ants.

Flying on a large commercial aircraft was okay, but Grant preferred flying in Papa's airplane, the *Mystery Girl*. Grant and his sister Christina liked to visit exciting places with their grandparents Mimi and Papa. Mimi wrote mystery books for children, and often brought the kids along as she traveled to research her stories.

"Did you see that big gold thing that looked like a mesa, Grant?" Christina asked, brushing her long brown hair away from her face as she gazed out the window from the seat in front of him.

"No," Grant replied. "I was sleeping. So what was it?"

"That was waste material from a gold mine," Papa said, as he set his black cowboy hat on his head. "South Africa is one of the leading producers of gold in the world. Johannesburg is also called 'Egoli,' or 'City of Gold.'"

Mimi smiled. "I like the sound of that," she said. "I do have a birthday coming up, and I do like gold jewelry," she added, winking at Papa.

"Wow," Christina said. "How deep are the mines?"

"Some of them are more than two miles deep," Papa replied. "Mining is very hard, dangerous work. So, my dear," he said, winking back at Mimi, "you need to appreciate all the hard work that went into your shiny gold jewelry!"

Christina whirled around in her seat to look at Mimi. "Are we going straight to Kruger National Park?" she asked.

"I'm not really sure," Mimi said, sliding her arm into her bright red jacket with sparkly rhinestones on the collar. "With our flight delay getting out of Atlanta, I think we arrived too late to get transportation to the park." Mimi turned around in her chair to look back at Papa, who was sitting next to Grant. "Do you know what the time is here, Papa?" she asked.

Papa looked at his watch and calculated the time difference in his head. "It should be about 5:30 local time," he replied.

Christina giggled. "It's time for Grant to fix his 'bed-head' hair," she said, pointing to Grant's messy blond curls.

"I've been sleeping!" Grant replied. "And I was all scrunched up in this seat. Who cares about hair anyway?" he grumbled, struggling to sit up in his makeshift bed of white airline pillows and blue blankets.

Suddenly, the flight attendant's voice filled the cabin.

"On behalf of our entire flight crew," she announced, "we would like to welcome you to Johannesburg, South Africa and thank you for flying with us today. The local time is 5:33 p.m. and we should be arriving at the gate shortly. Please remain seated until the seatbelt signs have been turned off." The flight attendant then repeated the same information in a language Grant and Christina had never heard.

"What language is that, Papa?" Grant asked.

"There are 11 recognized languages in South Africa," Papa replied. "English is mainly used for business, but it's not often used at home. I think she's speaking in isiZulu, which is spoken by about one quarter of South Africans."

"That's correct, Papa," Christina said. "That's exactly what it said in the South African guidebook I checked out of the library back home."

"Wow!" Grant said. "You're always right about everything, Papa! How do you do that?"

"Well, it's really quite easy," Papa replied. "I read a lot, pay attention to my surroundings, and try to plan ahead so I can be prepared for what might or might not happen," he explained. "There's nothing worse than being caught unaware."

"Unaware?" Grant asked, looking up at Papa with his big blue eyes.

"That means without warning or without proper planning," Christina jumped in.

"Oh," Grant said. "So, do we have any plans for tonight if we're not going to the park, or are we being caught unaware?"

"Grant," Mimi said with a chuckle. "Sometimes you just have to wing it. And that's what we'll do tonight. I'm sure we'll find something fun to do," she added.

As the seatbelt warning signs went out, Christina watched the passengers jump to their feet, pull their luggage out of the overhead bins, and wait to file off the plane.

"Guess this will take a while," Christina sighed, brushing the crumbs from her snack off her new blue jeans. She was ready to get going on their African adventure.

"Well," said Mimi, "it's taken us about 16 hours to get here, so a few more minutes won't hurt." She tousled Grant's blond curls. "That'll give us time to work on this hair!"

"Okay," Grant replied. "But I can't wait to get off this plane and get the ants out of my pants!"

FINDING
FOOD

"Bob! Bob! It's Herman," a man shouted in a strong South African accent, as Mimi and Papa struggled for position next to the luggage carousel in the baggage claim area of the airport. He pushed his way through the mass of people, waving furiously. Herman wore a tan safari suit and was only slightly taller than he was wide. He had a short, gray flat-top haircut, a bushy gray mustache, and he carried a cane, although he really didn't seem to be using it to get around.

Herman ran up to Papa and wrapped him in a friendly bear hug. "My friend, it has been years since I last saw you," Herman said, pulling away from Papa and gently grabbing Mimi's hand. "This must be your lovely bride," he added, kissing the back of Mimi's hand. "I am Dr. Herman Applegate, the game warden at Kruger National Park and your husband's college roommate!"

"Warden?" Grant asked. "Are the animals in prison?"

"Ah!" Dr. Applegate said. "You must be Grant. Your grandfather has told me about your inquisitive nature. I wouldn't call it a prison at all. The animals can move freely in the park, which covers 7,300 square miles. It is South Africa's largest wildlife reserve. I believe it's a wonderful place for the animals to live!"

Dr. Applegate noticed Christina behind Grant. "Christina, I'll bet," he remarked. "You are just as lovely a young lady as your grandfather described," he said.

Christina blushed and smiled, then quickly

Finding Food

closed her lips. She was self-conscious about the braces on her teeth. "Thank you," she replied. "I really like your accent. It sounds really cool."

Dr. Applegate laughed. "Many Americans comment on my accent," he said. "Some people tell me it sounds like a combination of a British accent and an Australian accent. But to me, it's just the way I talk. Now, I'll bet you two can't wait to go on a safari!"

"I don't know about Grant," Christina said, "but I can't wait to get started." She turned and poked her brother, who was busy looking around the terminal. "Grant?"

"Oh, yes," Grant said. "Me, too, but can we please eat first? My tummy is really talking to me!"

"Of course!" Dr. Applegate bellowed. "Bob, he's exactly like you—a man with a big appetite! Since it is too late to drive to the park, I've made reservations for you at my favorite hotel in Johannesburg. We'll go there after you eat."

Grant slowly moved behind the adults while Dr. Applegate, Papa, and Mimi discussed their plans. Christina stood next to Mimi, listening to the conversation intently.

There's got to be something edible in this airport, Grant thought, as he scanned the stores around the terminal. His eyes passed over a money kiosk similar to an ATM machine back home, but he couldn't see any restaurant or even a food court. He needed to find a snack - - and soon!

Grant noticed a tall black man with short-cropped hair looking in their direction. When he saw Grant staring at him, he bolted behind a thick round column. Grant moved further away from Papa and pretended he was looking somewhere else. He slowly gazed in the man's direction. The man suddenly emerged from behind the column and quickly blended into a crowd of passengers.

Grant saw something fall out of the man's jacket pocket and flutter to the floor just before the crowd swallowed him up. He scurried over and picked it up. It was a small white card with handwriting on it. Grant held the card up to look at it, but his eyes focused over the card's top edge at a rack filled with snacks. He stuffed the unread card into his back pocket and hurried over to the snack rack. His appetite made him forget all about the man and the card.

YOUR BASIC
CHEESEBURGER

Christina wiped her face with her napkin and leaned toward Grant. "Grant, you should have had the Chicken Schnitzel instead of a kid's cheeseburger," she said. "It was delicious."

"Hey," Grant said, "you can't go wrong with your basic cheeseburger. It always tastes good no matter what country you're in."

"My fish and chips just hit the spot," Mimi said, as she watched Papa finished his ostrich burger. "How was your meal, Papa?" she asked.

"Mmmm," Papa replied. "This ostrich tastes like very tender steak." He turned to Christina. "Want to try some?"

Christina wrinkled her nose. "I'll stick with my chicken, thanks," she said. As she reached for her glass of milk, Christina looked to her left, then to her right. At first, she had thought it was her imagination, but now she knew she was right. They were being watched! And it wasn't just by the servers who did a fabulous job of keeping their glasses full and their table clean.

The man watching them sat at a table across the room in a dark area of the restaurant. He was tall, black, and had short-cropped hair. He pretended to be enjoying his meal, but Christina could see that he was only faking it by the way he kept glancing at them.

The conversation at their table picked up as the plates where taken away. Dr. Applegate pointed their attention to various pictures along the wall that portrayed magnificent views of the South African coast and Kruger National Park.

He described each picture in vivid detail. As with the book on South Africa she had brought with her, Christina was enthralled by the beauty of this amazing country.

She had forgotten about the man watching them until Dr. Applegate stood to say goodnight. Christina spied the tall black man get up and cautiously follow Dr. Applegate out of the restaurant. *That was when she began to worry.*

SPY LIGHT

As Papa and Mimi checked in at the hotel desk, Christina grabbed Grant's bony elbow and pulled him aside. "Did you see that guy watching us in the restaurant?" she asked.

"You mean the one in the blue jeans, black t-shirt, and black leather jacket?" Grant asked.

"Apparently you did see him!" Christina exclaimed.

"I saw him in the airport, but not in the restaurant," Grant said. "So, if you saw him, and I saw him, we're definitely being watched!"

Grant suddenly remembered the white card and yanked it out of his back pocket. He waved it at Christina. "He dropped this."

"What does it say?" Christina asked.

"I don't know," Grant replied. "I haven't read it yet." He handed the card to Christina.

"Let's go, kids," Mimi said, whisking the kids into the elevator. "I am so tired I could sleep for a week!"

Christina quickly stuffed the card in her jacket pocket as the elevator doors shut behind her.

After Christina and Grant settled into bed, Papa and Mimi kissed them goodnight and went back into their connecting room. As soon as they were gone, Christina pulled the card out from under her pillow and held it under the flashlight she had borrowed from Grant's spy kit.

"Hey, that's mine!" Grant cried.

"Shhh!" Christina warned. "I'm just using it to read the card!"

"Okay," Grant replied. "But make sure you put it back with all my spy stuff!" He looked over at the door to Papa and Mimi's room. The light was still on so they wouldn't be able to see the flashlight beam. "What does it say?" he asked.

"It's a warning," Christina said. "It says,

BEWARE!
Try to stop us and you will never see her again!

"Whoa!" Grant whispered. "That doesn't sound like a warning. It sounds like a threat!"

"It sure does," Christina said. "There's something going on, because this is a serious threat. But," she continued, locking eyes with Grant, *"who's threatening who?"*

5

DAFFY DANCING

The next morning, the children were greeted by the sound of music and clapping as they stepped off the elevator with Mimi and Papa. "What's going on?" Christina asked.

"It's an African dance performance!" cried Mimi, ushering the children to the front of the crowd. Three African men dressed in animal skins and feather headdresses twirled around the hotel lobby to the pounding beat of traditional drums. Grant's mouth fell open in amazement.

"They're moving so fast!" he cried. The tallest dancer beckoned Grant and Christina to join him. Christina moved back, clutching Papa's arm. But Grant couldn't resist the invitation. He grabbed hold of the dancer's arm and began twisting and turning wildly to keep up with the rhythm. Mimi, Papa, and Christina roared with laughter.

CRASH! As he whirled and twirled, Grant suddenly toppled over, right into a potted palm tree. The tree toppled to the ground, flinging soil, palm fronds, and a little blond boy across the slick tile floor.

"Are you all right?" Mimi cried, pulling Grant to his feet.

Grant couldn't contain his giggles. "That...was...so...much...fun!" he panted. "I'm ready for the next song!"

Papa shook his head as he helped lift the palm tree back into its pot. "One performance is enough for today, pardner," he remarked. "We're going on a safari!"

Dr. Applegate joined them outside the lobby doors. "Bob," Dr. Applegate said to Papa, "I would love to join you for your ride to the park, but unfortunately I have other business to attend to."

"How are we getting to the park, Papa?" Grant asked.

Dr. Applegate patted Grant's head. "Normally," he said, "you would have to take the bus to the park. There, you would sign up to reserve a guide to take you and several other tourists through the park. But today, my private car will pick you up, and I've arranged for you to take a private safari with my two best guides."

"Wow!" Christina exclaimed. "That sounds better than being in a big group of people with just one guide. Thanks!"

"You are very welcome, my dear," Dr. Applegate replied. "And now I must be on my way. I shall see you all soon." He turned and walked back into the hotel.

"So, Papa," Grant said. "You and Dr. Applegate were roommates in college?"

"Yes, we were," Papa said, adjusting his cowboy hat. "When Mimi decided our next trip would be to South Africa," he continued, "I called him. That's when I found out he was now the game warden of a safari park. I knew Mimi wouldn't want to miss the chance to go on a real safari."

"Are we really going to hunt animals?" Grant said, his eyes growing wide.

"Oh, my, no!" Mimi cried. She shuddered as she wrapped her red shawl around her shoulders.

"I thought a safari was where you hunt ferocious wild animals, like lions and tigers, or elephants and rhinoceroses," Grant said.

"Some people do go on hunting safaris," Mimi explained, "but Kruger National Park is a reserve where you go on a safari to observe wild animals in their natural habitat. The park was actually established to protect animals from hunters. In fact," she added, "visitors to any park in South Africa have to pay a conservation fee to help preserve the park itself and the animals."

"Oh!" Grant said, a bit disappointed. "Why would we want to watch wild animals? That's like watching the kids at school eating lunch."

"Well," Papa replied with a chuckle, "we watch animals so we can learn about them. We watch how they live, how they survive, and how they care for their families. Observing an animal in its own natural habitat is better than seeing it in the zoo."

A shiny yellow Land Rover pulled up in front of the hotel. A man and a boy about Christina's age stepped out. The boy was slender with blond curly hair. He held up a poster-size white card with Papa's name written on it.

"There's our ride," Christina said, waving at the driver. But something else caught her eye. There was that man again, sitting in the back seat of a car parked in the hotel driveway! He looked at Christina and smiled.

It was the biggest smile Christina had ever seen. Sunlight reflected off a gold tooth in the front of his mouth. Suddenly, he turned away from the window and the car pulled away, quickly disappearing into traffic.

A chill slithered up Christina's spine.

6

EXOTIC ANIMALS

After storing their luggage, the family piled into the Land Rover. The boy climbed in back with Christina and Grant, while Mimi and Papa sat up front with the man.

"Hi," the boy said. "My name is Bindley Sangster, but you can call me Bino." Bino pointed at the driver. "That's my father. He's the best guide in all of South Africa! He's also a wildlife photographer."

"Hi," Grant said. "I'm Grant, and this is Christina." Grant pointed at Mimi and Papa.

"Those are our grandparents, Mimi and Papa, and we're the best tourists in all of South Africa!"

"Does your father take pictures for a magazine?" Christina asked.

"Actually," Bino replied, "he takes pictures for lots of magazines. He's a freelance photographer. Right now, he has an assignment from the Smithsonian Museum of Natural History in your country. He takes most of his pictures while guiding safaris."

"I am quite impressed," Mimi said, smiling at Bino's father. "That's a very famous and important museum! You must take magnificent pictures."

"Thank you," Mr. Sangster replied. "I love what I do."

"Well, I hope we see lots of animals today!" Grant cried. He glanced out the window at the soothing landscape of waving grass dotted with trees. The sky, without a cloud in it, was the most beautiful blue color Grant had ever seen. "Hey! What are those?" he asked, pointing at a galloping herd that looked like deer.

"Those are impala," Bino replied. "They are *everywhere* in the park; just everywhere." He laughed. "Lots of people refer to them as the 'McDonald's' of the African plain."

Christina and Grant looked puzzled. "Why?" Christina asked.

"Because," Bino replied, "they are easy, quick food for predators, and they have a big 'M' on their backsides! Take a look!"

Christina and Grant watched the impala herd sprint away from their Land Rover, and then burst out laughing. "It looks like someone painted 'M's' on them," Christina observed, "impala after impala after impala, without missing one!"

After a few minutes, Grant noticed Christina looking out the back window. "Is there something behind us, Christina?"

"Uh," Christina said, turning around and looking at Mimi and Papa in the front seat. They were deep in conversation with Bino's father. "Grant," she whispered, "I saw him again this morning. He was sitting in a car in the hotel driveway, and he gave me this big, fiendish smile before his car sped away."

"Saw who?" Bino asked.

"Some guy who has been following us," Grant said. "Christina thinks something strange is going on. Woooo," Grant added, moving his hands all around his head.

"Strange, how strange?" Bino asked, frowning at Christina.

"Grant saw him first at the airport, then I spotted him last night watching us while we ate dinner," Christina whispered, pulling the card out of her pocket. "This fell out of his pocket at the airport."

Bino took the card from Christina and read it. "Hmm," he said. "Maybe it was not meant for you and maybe you are not who he is watching."

"Then who is he watching?" Grant asked. "We were the only ones there."

"Not exactly, Grant," Christina said. "Dr. Applegate was with us at the airport and at dinner last night. Bino, do you think this threat could be for him?"

"It could be," Bino said. "I've heard that there are poachers, or animal thieves, at the park. I've noticed that some of the animals I saw last year are not coming around this year."

"You know the animals that closely that you can tell when one is missing?" Christina asked.

"Kind of," Bino said. "There are some that we see all the time. You get to recognize them. There are several missing, including Bukekayo."

"What type of animal is that?" Grant asked.

"Bukekayo means 'beautiful' in Zulu," Bino said. "She's a white lion, so she is very rare. She is also Dr. Applegate's pride and joy. Everyone thought white lions had become extinct in the wild until Bukekayo showed up as a cub several years ago. Since then she has had several litters of white lion cubs. I have spotted her cubs, but I haven't seen her in the last several weeks."

"That's terrible," Christina said, checking to see if the three adults were still talking. "Why would someone steal animals? They certainly wouldn't use them as food, would they?"

"No, not as food," Bino whispered. "They steal them to sell on the exotic animal black market. Believe it or not, there are people, carnivals, and even circuses, around the world that will pay a lot of money for leopards, elephants, lions, and African exotic birds."

"What's a black market?" Grant asked.

"It's an operation where things are sold and bought illegally," Bino explained.

Mimi suddenly turned around. "Did I hear you talking about exotic birds?" she asked. "What about exotic birds?"

"Bino was telling us about all the different animals in the park," Grant said.

"Yes," Bino said. "I was just about to tell them we will stay overnight at the luxurious

Hoyo Hoyo Tsonga Lodge in one of the six traditional Tsonga huts. Then we'll get an early start in the morning."

"An early start?" said Mimi. "How early?" After all, this was her vacation!

"About 6 a.m.," Bino said. "Our vehicles are already loaded. As soon as we arrive at our campsite, we will set up camp and then you will be ready to enjoy 'roughing it' on your five-day camping trip through the African wilderness."

"What?!?" both Mimi and Christina cried. "Five days?"

A REAL
SAFARI

"Hold on," Grant said. "You mean we're going on a real safari and not one of those fancy tourist safaris?"

"Oh, yes," Bino replied. "You will get really close to the animals. You will love it."

"Cool," Grant said, noticing Mimi looked a bit concerned. She turned back around and joined the conversation between Papa and Bino's father.

"So what do you mean by 'roughing it'?" Christina asked.

"Your grandfather had originally planned for you to go on the Spirit of Adventure Safari, which is nice, but a little boring for me," Bino replied. "Because Dr. Applegate is a good friend of your grandfather, he asked my father and another guide, Baruti, to take you on a real safari. We will bring everything we need to eat. And we'll bring plenty of water to drink, so we don't **dehydrate**."

Christina's eyes grew wide. "Well, that's a relief!"

"Cool!" Grant exclaimed. "Will we have any weapons? I'm pretty good with a bow and arrow, you know. Watch this!" Grant imitated shooting a bow and arrow at the car next to them.

"No," Bino said. "We will not have weapons, but my father and Baruti will. You just never know when you might come face to face with one of Africa's Big Five and have to defend yourself. To be truthful, my father is so careful that he has only had to shoot one wild animal since he started working here."

"Africa's Big Five?" Christina asked. "What are they?"

"From biggest to smallest," Bino replied, "the Big Five are the elephant, rhinoceros, water buffalo, lion, and leopard."

"Do you think we'll be able to see all of them?" Grant asked, sitting up expectantly in his seat.

"Well, maybe," Bino said. "The leopards are hard to find, but we may be able to see the water buffalo at the watering hole near the lodge tonight, or maybe some elephants. Mandisa and I will show you around once you have settled into your hut."

"Mandisa?" Christina asked. "Who is that?"

"Mandisa is my best friend and the daughter of one of the park's administrators," Bino replied.

"Will she be coming on the safari with us?" Christina asked.

"She wouldn't miss it for all the lemon drops in the world," Bino said.

"Lemon drops?" Christina repeated.

"Oh, yes," Bino said. "Mandisa loves lemon drops. She always has some with her."

"Cool," Grant remarked. "I like anyone who likes candy! Is she South African?"

"Yes, she is Tsonga," Bino said. "They are indigenous to this area."

"Oh, so she's a genius?" Grant asked. "Some people say I'm pretty smart, too," he added, sitting taller in his seat.

"No, Grant, 'indigenous' means that her ancestors are from this part of South Africa," Christina said.

Christina laid back in her seat. "Great," she mumbled. "Camping in the wild, elephants, rhinos, and lions, plus now we have to solve the mystery of the missing animals."

"Mandisa and I will help you," Bino said.

"But where do we start?" Christina said.

"The same way we always do," Grant said. "*We follow the clues!*"

LUXURIOUS LODGE

Christina was thrilled at the first stop on her safari journey once she got a look at the luxurious air-conditioned huts at the Hoyo Hoyo Tsonga Lodge. She loved the fluffy, king-size beds, the antique baths, and the smiling staff dressed in traditional Tsonga clothing. She couldn't believe they were going to leave this beautiful place to go camping in the wilderness!

Grant paced the hut like a caged animal. "I'm bored," he announced. "What's to do here?"

WHAM!

THWACK!

"What was that?" Grant asked, running over to the window. "Christina! LOOK!" he cried, shoving the thick green drapes aside.

Tree limbs whacked the windows as a family of three elephants passed by on a nearby trail, their enormous ears flapping against their massive necks. Clouds of dust arose behind them.

"They are HUGE!" Christina exclaimed. "And look at the little one trying to keep up. He is so cute!"

Mimi joined the children at the window. "I just knew we would see some elephants," she remarked. "This lodge is located on an ancient elephant trail. What a treat!"

Luxurious Lodge

KNOCK!
KNOCK!

The visitors were jolted back to reality by someone knocking on the hut's thick wooden door. Grant saw Mimi moving toward the door to answer it and shot past her. "I'll get it, Mimi," he said. "It's probably Bino and Mandisa, anyway."

Grant opened the door. A hefty black man filled the entire doorway.

"Hi," the man said, bending down and thrusting out his hand to shake Grant's hand. "I am Baruti, your guide for your trek into the African wilderness."

Grant reached out and shook Baruti's massive hand just as Bino and a pretty young girl slid by him and entered the hut. Baruti ducked under the low doorway and followed them inside.

"Grant and Christina," Bino said, "this is Mandisa."

Christina noticed that they were about the same size, although Mandisa was closer to Grant's age. She found herself staring at Mandisa's smooth ebony skin and sparkling smile. Her hair fell in tight ringlets around her head.

Papa walked into the room as they all shook hands. "Baruti," he said, "I'm glad you could come by. Is there anything we need to do before we leave in the morning?"

While Papa and Baruti talked, Grant pulled Mimi aside. "Is it okay if Christina and I go out with Bino and Mandisa?" he asked.

"Yes," Mimi said. "But don't go far, and get back here before sunset. I don't want you wandering around in the dark."

"Okay," Grant said, hustling the other three children out the door before Mimi changed her mind!

MONKEY PARADE

"Mandisa, did Bino tell you about the note?" Grant asked, after they had cleared the hut.

"Yes," Mandisa said, "but it doesn't really tell us much."

"Well, let's think about this," Christina said. "If the note was meant for Dr. Applegate, and it is from animal thieves like we believe, then 'Try to stop us and you will never see her again' must be referring to Bukekayo, Dr. Applegate's favorite lion."

"I hadn't thought of that," Bino said.

"Not only that," Christina added, "but it also tells us that Dr. Applegate has uncovered what they are doing and has tried to stop them from stealing the animals."

"What makes you think that?" Mandisa asked.

"The first few words of the threat," Grant said, "that talked about trying to stop them. They wouldn't say that if someone wasn't on to their scheme."

"Okay," Bino said, "but does that help us?"

"It tells us that Dr. Applegate knows something," Christina explained. "Is he here today?"

"No," Mandisa said. "I passed by his office at the administration building earlier, and my father said he was away on business."

"Hmm," Christina said, smiling at Grant. "Are you thinking what I'm thinking?"

"Yes," Grant said. "Great minds think alike! Mandisa, can you take us to the administration building?"

"Yes," said Mandisa. "But why?"

"We may be able to find some clues in Dr. Applegate's office," Christina said.

Mandisa thought about it for a moment and looked at her wristwatch. "That shouldn't be a problem," she said. "Everyone except my father has gone home by now. Follow me, it is a short walk through that grove of trees." Mandisa pointed at a thick wooded area beyond the brush and grass of the savanna.

Grant followed Christina, Bino, and Mandisa through the trees. The warm African air felt thick and hot, but had a clean, fresh smell. As they entered the woods between the lodge and administration building, Grant and Christina were startled by a chattering sound in the trees above them.

"What's all the noise?" Grant asked.

"That's not noise," Bino said. "Those are monkeys. Be careful, they like to throw things."

"Throw things!" Grant said. "Like what?"

Grant looked up to see a reddish-green mango miss his head by inches. "Hey!" Grant cried, putting his hands on his skinny hips and glaring at a group of chattering monkeys in the trees above him. "What did you do that for?"

"Those are vervet monkeys," Bino said. "They can be mean, but are usually playful."

"I'll play!" Grant declared, as he picked up the mango, wiped it on his shirt, and took a big, juicy bite. "Yum, these are a lot sweeter than the ones back home. Try it, Christina."

As Christina grabbed the fruit, Grant saw a tiny monkey throw another mango. Grant reached up and caught it. "So, do you want to play catch?" he asked, raising his arm to throw the mango.

AIEEEEEEEEEE!

The monkey shrieked and leaped up and down on a swaying tree limb. It suddenly stopped and stared at Grant.

"Is the fact that he's staring at me good or bad?" Grant asked.

"Hmm," Bino said. "I am not sure!"

EEEEKKK! EEEEKKK! HOOO! HOOO!

High-pitched squeals pierced the air. The monkeys dropped their fruit and began to jump and swing from tree to tree.

"What's going on?" Christina asked, watching as 30 or 40 frantic monkeys appeared above them.

"They sense a predator is nearby," Mandisa said. "See how the mothers cradle their young to protect them from being taken?"

"I'll bet you it is a bateleur eagle," Bino said. "They hunt vervet monkeys, especially the young ones."

"Oh, no!" Christina cried.

Grant couldn't take his eyes off the shrieking monkeys swinging from tree to tree above him. "It looks like a monkey parade up there!"

The monkeys swung through the trees, chattering frantically as they moved.

"There it is!" Mandisa said, pointing to a majestic eagle with a fuzzy black head and crimson beak swooping down out of the sky. "Bino, you were right!   They were afraid of an eagle!"

"Eagles d-d-don't eat people, d-d-do they?" Christina asked, noticing the razor-sharp claws on the eagle's feet as it flew straight toward the monkeys.

"That depends," Bino said.   "Do you taste like monkey?"

HIDE AND SEEK

"This is the administration building?" Grant said. "It looks more like an African version of an American farmhouse."

"I believe it was something like that a long time ago," Mandisa said. "But now, all of the park's business activities take place here. Dr. Applegate's office is over here."

The children followed Mandisa to an office door with Dr. Applegate's name on it. The sparse office had just a desk, several filing cabinets, and an old leather couch in it.

"What are we looking for?" Bino asked.

"Clues," Christina said.

"You mean like this?" Bino said, holding up a card like the one Grant had found at the airport.

"What does it say?" Christina asked.

Bino handed the card to Christina. She read,

Don't try to uncover who we are. Just do what we say or you'll be sorry!

"Whoa," Grant said. "Another threat!"

"It also sounds like Dr. Applegate has been trying to discover who these people are," Christina said.

"Bino," Grant said, "where did you find that?"

"In the desk's center drawer," Bino said.

Christina joined him and ran her hand under the desk drawer. "Here's something else," she said, removing an envelope from the underside of the drawer. She carefully opened it and fingered through its contents.

"They're receipts for animal sales to carnivals and other people," Christina said, pulling the papers from the envelope.

"What kind of animals?" Mandisa asked.

"Well," Christina replied, shuffling through the receipts, "it looks like leopards, birds, elephants, and one white lion!"

"Oh, no," Bino said. "Dr. Applegate's going to be upset when he finds out they sold Bukekayo."

"I wouldn't count on that," Christina said, flicking through each receipt. "It looks like Dr.

Applegate signed the receipts to sell each one of these animals!"

"No!" Mandisa said, grabbing a receipt out of Christina's hand. "That is impossible! He would never sell Bukekayo."

"Even if it meant he would get a lot of money?" Christina said. "Because these receipts look like they add up to almost one million dollars!"

CLOMP!

CLOMP!

CLOMP!

Suddenly, the children heard footsteps and soft voices in the hallway. Mandisa stuffed the white lion receipt in her pocket. Christina slid the pile of receipts into the envelope. Before she could put them back under the desk, Bino pulled her and Mandisa through a side door into another office.

Grant hurried after them. As he began to move, he spotted the corner of a small white card barely sticking out from under the desk calendar. He grabbed it and then ran into the other room, quietly closing the door behind him.

Bino and Mandisa slid inside a tiny closet and shut the door. Christina crouched behind an African sculpture in the corner of the room. The only place left for Grant was under the desk. He quickly slid under it and pulled the chair back in behind him.

EVERY SQUARE INCH!

The children sat motionless in their hiding places as a group of people entered Dr. Applegate's office.

"This is not possible," Mandisa heard her father say. "Dr. Applegate would never do anything illegal. He's a good man, inspector."

"So you say," the inspector said, "but others say different. They say he's guilty."

"Who are these others and what are they saying about Herman?" Mandisa's father demanded.

"Who they are doesn't matter," the inspector replied. "What they say is that he has been selling exotic animals, poached from this park, on the black market." The inspector looked down his glasses at the man in front of him. "They say the evidence is in this office." He looked at the two other men who came with him. "Examine every square inch," the inspector told them.

The men yanked open file cabinets and littered the floor with papers as they looked for evidence to link Dr. Applegate to the crime. The inspector looked around the room and noticed the door to the other office. "Where does that go?" he asked.

"It's an unused office," Mandisa's father said.

CRREEEEEEK!

The inspector opened the door and looked inside the sparsely furnished room. He stepped over to the sculpture to admire it. He walked behind the desk and looked out the window. The noise in Dr. Applegate's office increased as the men became angry that they hadn't found anything yet. The inspector pushed the window open all the way and felt the humid breeze waft across his face.

Grant could see the inspector's legs. In fact, he could probably reach out and touch them! The inspector suddenly turned in Grant's direction and yanked open one of the desk drawers. It was empty. He pulled open another and still found nothing. He whipped the chair backwards and sat down in it. His polished shoes moved to within an inch of Grant's bottom.

Grant held his breath, as he heard more shoes enter the room.

"Inspector," a man said, "we have searched everything. There is nothing."

The inspector pushed the chair out to stand up. His toes slid forward a fraction of an inch and then back out from under the desk. Grant bit his lip. The inspector stood and handed Mandisa's father a card. "Have Dr. Applegate call me when he gets back," he said, as he headed for the door.

Mandisa's father looked at the mess in Applegate's office. Files and desk drawers were piled on top of the hill of paper reports. "What about his office?" he shouted after the inspector.

Without looking back, the inspector said, "He knows where everything goes."

As their footsteps receded into the distance, Mandisa's father grabbed the phone on the desk above Grant's head and dialed a number.

"They've left," he said, "but not before destroying your office. Like you said, there was nothing to find. They want you to call as soon as you return."

Mandisa's father listened to Dr. Applegate as he spoke.

"Yes," he said. "I will take care of it quickly." He hung up the phone and walked briskly out of the office, closing the door behind him.

RUN FOR IT!

Grant counted to 60 slowly and then climbed out from under the desk. He peeked at the mess in Dr. Applegate's office. "Whoa," he said. "Glad I don't have to clean that mess up! That's worse than my bedroom!" He moved toward the door and looked down the hallway. No one was there. "Okay, guys you can come out," he said.

Bino and Mandisa burst out of the closet. "That was close," Bino said.

Mandisa remained quiet.

"Well," Christina said. "We're in the middle of this now. I think we may have what they wanted!" She waved the envelope containing the receipts.

"My father," Mandisa said. "Is he involved in a crime?"

"Your father will be okay, Mandisa, and so will Dr. Applegate," Grant said.

"What do you mean, Grant?" Christina said. "We have the evidence."

"Do we?" Grant said. "Or do we have evidence someone planted to make Dr. Applegate look guilty?" Grant walked into Dr. Applegate's office and rummaged through the papers until he found one with Dr. Applegate's signature on it.

"Mandisa, do you still have that receipt?" he asked.

"Yes," Mandisa said, removing it from her pocket and giving it to Grant.

"Ha," Grant said, comparing the two signatures. "Just as I thought, the signatures don't match."

Christina, Bino, and Mandisa examined the signatures too.

"How did you know they wouldn't match?" Bino asked.

Christina hit herself in the forehead with the palm of her hand. "Grant figured it out!" she cried. "Grant noticed that when your father was on the phone, he said to Dr. Applegate, 'Just like you said, there was nothing to find.' Dr. Applegate wouldn't have said that if he had hidden the receipts under the desk drawer."

"Oh," Mandisa said. "So, who hid the receipts there?"

Grant pulled the card from his pocket. "I found this just before running in here," he said, handing the card to Christina.

It was blank on one side. The other side read,

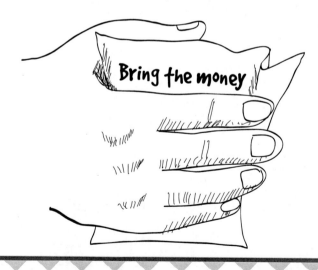

Christina was interrupted by footsteps in the hall again.

Bino whispered, "Run for it! Out the window!" Within seconds, they were out of the room and racing toward the grove of trees.

VERY BRAVE OR VERY FOOLISH

As the Land Rover rolled across the endless savanna, Christina and Grant were mesmerized by the sea of grass and the animals that lived there. Herds of impala thundered across the horizon. Birds burst out of trees in a frenzy as the Land Rover disturbed their rest. Elephants gracefully sauntered under the shade of a baobab tree.

"Look at the giraffes!" Christina cried, her eyes glued to the graceful animals lumbering across the road in front of them. "I can't believe they are so close to us! They look like they are really tame and friendly," she added.

"I wonder how long it takes them to swallow a lemon drop," Grant remarked. "It's a long way down that throat!"

"Are you children okay?" Baruti asked, as he parked his vehicle behind the Land Rover carrying Bino's father, Papa, and Mimi. The vehicle had stopped, and Mr. Sangster was stepping out of it with his camera.

"We're great!" Grant almost shouted. "This is way better than any zoo!" He craned his neck to see what was happening up ahead. "Why are we stopping?" he asked.

"My dad is taking some pictures," Bino explained. "It's not so easy to photograph these animals. They hear you coming and run away, so lots of times all he gets are shots of their rear ends!"

Grant giggled. Christina frowned at him. "Don't get started with your bathroom humor!" she warned.

"But..." Grant replied, "but..." He couldn't contain his giggles.

The vehicles started up again, and moved to their next stop, a ledge overlooking a small ravine with tall, dry grass and a shady baobab tree. Mimi and Papa climbed out before the children did.

"What are they looking at?" Grant asked.

"I don't know," Baruti replied.

"Let's find out," Grant said. Before Baruti could say anything, Grant jumped out the door and ran toward the ravine.

Papa and Mimi saw him coming and waved him back toward the Land Rover, but his curiosity kept him moving toward the ravine. Then he heard them shouting, "Grant! Grant! Get back in the vehicle! GRANT!"

As he peered over the edge of the ravine, he thought it was his imagination as the tan grass began to move. But suddenly, he could make out the distinct features of a lion's head, and saw the razor sharp teeth in its wide-open mouth.

The roar was louder than anything Grant had heard in his entire life! He felt the air around him change as the sound of the lion's roar passed over him. He wanted to run, but instead stared into the lion's dark gray eyes. In the background, he heard Mimi and Christina pleading with him to get back.

The cocking of Bino's father's rifle brought him out of his trance. But he kept his eyes locked on the lion's. The lion paced back and forth, but never charged toward him. After a few seconds, it turned and stalked back into the brush. "Back away, Grant," said Mr. Sangster. "Slowly."

Grant backed away from the ravine, but never took his eyes off the retreating lion. Mimi grabbed him as soon as the lion had disappeared. Grant slumped in her arms, his legs feeling like they were full of jelly.

Papa was relieved, but angry. "Boy, you get your behind back in that vehicle and don't get out of it again until you are told to do so. You about scared your grandmother and me half to death."

Mimi was breathing hard with her hand on her chest.

"I'm sorry, Mimi," Grant said. "I just wanted to see what you were all looking at."

Mimi took a deep breath and relaxed a little. "Don't ever do that again, Grant," she sighed. "Now, do what your grandfather told you."

"Yes, ma'am," Grant said. He turned and ran back to the Land Rover.

"Man," Bino said, "you are one crazy American. You just faced down the king of the jungle and walked away from him. Wow!"

Grant noticed the smell of lemons and saw Mandisa tossing a lemon drop into her mouth. She held out a couple for him, and he took them. As he turned forward, he saw Baruti set his rifle down on the seat next to him.

"I know your grandfather already spoke to you," Baruti said, "but when you are on a safari, you need to be aware of the fact that danger may be lurking behind every tree or in the brush all around you. The first time you drop your guard may be your last."

"Yes, sir!" Grant said.

"With that said," Baruti said, "I have never seen a man stare down a lion, let alone a boy. You are either very brave or very foolish. I hope you know the difference between the two."

WHO DONE IT?

The only light in the children's tent, which sat on a raised platform to keep lizards and snakes from getting to them, came from a small battery-powered lantern.   After entering the tent, Christina reached back and zipped the mosquito screen closed.

"Finally," Bino said.   "I thought we'd never get a chance to talk about the card Grant found in Dr. Applegate's office."

"Yeah," Grant said.   "They've kept us pretty busy all day."

"Before we get started," Mandisa remarked, "does anyone want a snack?"

"Sure," Christina said. "I am pretty hungry."

"Me, too," Grant added.

Mandisa pulled out a snack bag and reached inside it. Christina read the outside label. "Mopani worms. Mopani worms?" she cried, grimacing. "How can you eat worms?"

"They're good!" Bino declared, popping two worms into his mouth. "A mopani worm is the caterpillar of the emperor moth, which is one of the largest moths in the world. The biggest ones are the best because they contain more fat. Come on, try one," he continued, motioning to Grant.

"Oh, okay," Grant said. "I'm not afraid of bugs." To Christina's horror, Grant picked the biggest one he could find in Mandisa's bag and took a bite. He paused, then wrinkled his nose. "They're not bad," he said, smacking his lips, "but they're not good, either. Tastes kind of like fish."

Christina shuddered. "Yuck!" she exclaimed. "Double yuck! I'll just take a few lemon drops, please." She popped the candy into her mouth. "Now," she said, "let's get down to business." She whipped the card out of her pocket and read,

Bring the money tomorrow at dusk. Drop it at her favorite watering hole. That way nobody gets hurt, man or lion.

"What does that mean?" Mandisa asked.

"Hmm," Bino said. "It looks like instead of selling Bukekayo on the black market, the animal thieves have decided to sell her back to Dr. Applegate for ransom!"

"Do you think Dr. Applegate knows who the thieves are?" Mandisa asked.

"I've been thinking about it," Christina said. "And I think whoever tried to frame Dr. Applegate has to be close to him. At least close enough to be able to get into his office and plant evidence."

"I have a question," Mandisa demanded, hands on hips. "Why do you care who put Dr. Applegate's picture in a frame? Why do you keep talking about framing him?"

Bino laughed. "Sorry, Mandisa," he said. "We need to explain. To frame someone means to make it look like he committed a crime that he did not commit."

"Oh," Mandisa replied. "So you think someone is trying to make it look like Dr. Applegate sold the animals, but he really didn't?"

"Exactly!" Christina replied. "We're trying to figure out who might **conspire** against him!"

15

YOU'VE
BEEN
WARNED!

As Bino, Grant, and Mandisa washed down their mopani worm snack with chilled bottles of water, Grant thought about the card he found in Dr. Applegate's office. "That must have been a warning to Dr. Applegate," he remarked.

"A warning?" Mandisa said.

"Yes," Grant said, pointing at the card in Christina's hand. "The note warned they could hurt Bukekayo and Dr. Applegate if he didn't cooperate."

"I agree," Christina said.

"There's another thing I haven't had the chance to tell you," Grant said. "I saw the same man we saw at the airport and restaurant outside Dr. Applegate's window hiding behind a small grass hut."

"Did he see you?" Christina asked.

"No," Grant said. "And he was gone by the time we left."

"Ha!" Bino said. "That proves he was after Dr. Applegate. He probably planted those receipts."

"If he is one of the thieves," Mandisa said, popping another lemon drop in her mouth, "then he probably saw us go into the building, even if he could not see us in Dr. Applegate's office."

"True," Christina said. "But, he may have figured we were there to see your dad or even Dr. Applegate."

"What's that?" Grant said, hearing a rustling noise.

"Let's go see," Bino remarked.

The children hopped to their feet. Grant held the light out in front of him as they entered the sleeping area of the tent.

Grant shined the light around the whole tent. Nothing. Out of the corner of his eye, he saw something move. Suddenly, Bino yanked him backwards. "Watch out!" he cried.

A poisonous puff adder snake struck at Grant.

Grant yelled. Bino shook his head.

"We don't kill snakes," Bino said. "They have their purpose."

"Then let's get out of here!" Grant shouted, stumbling as fast as he could to the front portion of the tent. He almost ran over Christina and Mandisa, who scrambled to keep up with him.

"Stand still!" Bino ordered. He reached into his pocket and pulled out a small version of a gourd flute. He blew into one end of the small flute and a high-pitched rhythmic tune filled the tent. Bino began moving the flute back and forth. The snake became mesmerized and started swaying to the music.

Bino motioned for the kids to move against the tent wall and out of the tent. Once outside, Christina, Mandisa and Grant hurried over to a nearby Land Rover to watch what Bino did next.

Bino led the snake out of the tent and into the brush. As it slithered away, he dropped to his knees and wiped the sweat off his forehead with his sleeve.

"That was a close one!" he whispered. "A very close call for my American friends!"

You've Been Warned!

< 85 >

IT'S ALL IN THE NUMBERS

The sun burned high overhead without a cloud in sight to soften its intense heat. Grant pulled one of Papa's bandanas out of his pocket to wipe the sweat off his neck.

The group had been out on safari all morning and had already seen antelope, giraffes, water buffalo, bushbucks, jackals, and kudus. Mr. Sangster had stopped Mimi and Papa's Land Rover several times to snap pictures for his latest assignment.

The vehicles rested at the top of a crest near a watering hole where they watched the animals come and go. Christina was amazed at how two elephants, four baboons, a couple of hyenas, and five storks shared a long drink of water in peace.

Grant and Bino stood in the back of the Land Rover watching the animals.

"That was pretty cool how you handled that snake last night," Grant said. "Where did you learn to do that?"

"I have an uncle who is a snake charmer in Tunisia in northern Africa," Bino replied. "We visited him last summer and he taught me the basics of snake charming. Actually, snakes cannot hear the music. It is the back and forth motion that calms them down."

"Well," Grant said, "that just goes to prove Papa's idea about not being caught unaware. Everything we learn may come in handy someday!" Grant watched a baboon scoop water from the watering hole with his hand as a hyena moved behind him.

Bino said, "Watch this."

The hyena slowly tiptoed within a few feet of the baboon. It sat back, ready to spring on its unsuspecting prey, when suddenly the baboon spun around and pounded its fist on the top of the hyena's head. The hyena jumped back and whimpered as it backed away.

Grant roared with laughter. "That was so funny!" he cried, holding his stomach. "Attack of the baboon!"

"Most hyenas are a lot smarter than that one," Bino said, leaning back against the rooftop. "Do you see many animals where you live?"

"Some," Grant said, "but not like this! In my town in Georgia, we see raccoons and deer and squirrels. That's about it." Grant scanned the distance to see if any more animals were coming to the watering hole. Two giraffes slowly lumbered over, their heads bobbing above the trees. "Oh, and snakes, too," he added. "And lots of bugs."

Suddenly, Bino stood up perfectly straight and pointed to the watering hole. "Grant," he whispered, "look at the water. Do you see the gentle vibrations in it?"

"I think I can see it," Grant said. "Why?"

"Because it means a rhino stampede is coming our way," Bino replied. At that very moment, his father and Baruti motioned for everyone to get back to their vehicles.

Suddenly, the ground began to rumble beneath their feet. A massive cloud of dust in the distance rose above a crash of black rhinos thundering across the savanna. The sound was deafening!

"Why are they doing that?" Grant yelled.

"Something must have spooked them," Bino shouted back. "Just be glad we're over here and they are over there!"

Christina and Mandisa stuck their heads out of the front of the Land Rover, holding bandanas over their mouths and noses to shut out the dust. "Is it over yet?" Christina asked. "That's one of the loudest things I have ever heard in my life!"

"Yes, they are past us now," Bino replied, as Mimi and Papa came over to check on the kids. "Those are black rhinos," he explained. "There are 5,000 black and white rhinos in the park."

"5,000?" Grant said. "Wow, that's a lot of rhinos. How many lions does the park have?"

"Close to 1,500," Bino said.

Christina and Mandisa squeezed up through the rooftop hole. "Now what are you guys talking about?" Christina asked.

"Bino was telling me how many lions are in the park," Grant said.

"Oh, I love this," Mandisa said. "Ask him how many reptiles are in the park."

"Okay," Grant said. "Bino, how many reptile species are in the park?"

"Easy," Bino said. "114."

"Hmm," Grant said. "Amphibians?"

Bino yawned. "34."

"Buffalo?" Grant asked.

"2,500," Bino said.

"Elephants?" Grant tried to stump Bino.

"Believe it or not," Bino said, "12,000."

"I got you this time," Grant said, smiling. "How many trees?"

"Easy," Bino said. "336 varieties."

"Leopards?" Grant asked.

"1,000," Bino said. "Give or take a few."

"Fish?" Grant asked.

"There are 49 different species of fish in the park's rivers," Bino said.

"Okay," Grant said, thinking he had him this time. "Birds?"

"Around 507 species," Bino replied. "Some of them can only be found here and not anywhere else in the world."

"Wow," Grant said. "You know this park really well! Can you take my next math test for me?"

WATERING HOLE

The kids piled back into the Land Rover to continue their safari.

Mandisa was still thinking about the poachers in the park. "Do you think they know that we're on their trail?" she asked, twirling a lemon drop around in her mouth.

"I don't know for sure," Christina remarked. "But we need to be careful about what we say and do."

"Well," Grant remarked, "it'll be over after tonight once Dr. Applegate pays the ransom and they release Bukekayo."

"That is true," Bino said, "but it will not stop them from poaching. If anything, it will encourage them more."

"The card said to drop the money at her favorite watering hole," Grant said. "Do you know where that is located?"

"Yes!" Bino replied. "It is about 20 kilometers north of here, near Sable Sleepover Hide. The watering hole overlooks the Sable Dam. Many animals gather there for water."

"Sable Sleepover Hide?" Christina said.

"Yes," Bino said. "It is kind of a sleepover stop for campers. But, it's very primitive. There's no electricity and guests have to bring their own food and water."

"So, we just have to get there, hide out, and watch who comes to retrieve the bag of money," Grant said. "So, how do we get Baruti to take us there?"

"I do not think he will," Mandisa said. "I am sure he mapped out this safari long before now. He would need a good reason to suddenly change it."

"Okay, so where are we supposed to be going next?" Christina said. "Maybe it's close to the watering hole."

Bino pulled out the list of stops that Baruti had given to him yesterday. "Oh, wow," Bino said. "You are not going to believe this! We are supposed to stop near Bukekayo's watering hole at dusk this evening!"

"Wow!" Christina cried. *"And you know what that means!"*

SHAKE, RATTLE, AND ROLL

"IIII ddonn'ttt llliikke thisss," Christina remarked, as the Land Rover bumped and bounced over the rough terrain. The access road to Sable Hide was a narrow, tightly twisting path around a rugged mountainside.

"III ffeeell lllikke aaa mmiillkksshakkke," Grant said.

"Mmmee, ttooo," Bino added.

"Lleemmoonnn ddropp aanyoonee?" Mandisa said, holding out the shaking box of candy.

The road smoothed out for a short stretch. "Oh, that's better," Christina said, noticing that she couldn't see Papa and Mimi's vehicle in front

of them any more.

The radio by Baruti's side clicked and **emitted** some static. Finally, Mr. Sangster's voice rang out. "Baruti, are you okay?" he said. "I've lost sight of you."

"Yes," Baruti replied. "I've slowed down a little because the children were having a rough ride. We should catch up soon."

"Okay," said Bino's father. "We will wait by the Hide for you."

"Sounds good," Baruti replied. "We will see you soon."

Baruti waited to hear Mr. Sangster say more. When he didn't, he set the radio down on the seat beside him. Grant heard a distinct click.

Baruti had turned the radio off.

"Mr. Baruti," Grant started to say, "why did you...?"

A loud noise, plus screams from the girls stopped Grant in mid sentence. A jagged boulder tumbled down the mountain and landed right in front of the Land Rover. Baruti hit the brakes and the back end of the vehicle spun out to the left. The Land Rover skidded sideways toward the boulder, stopping just a few inches from it.

The front end of the Land Rover now faced the mountainside. Grant looked out the window and saw another boulder heading right for them!

"Get down!" Grant shouted, jumping on his sister and Mandisa and pushing them to the floor.

The boulder landed right behind the Land Rover, trapping it between the boulders. The kids noticed that Baruti had hit his head on the windshield and was not moving. Bino leaned over and checked his pulse.

"He's unconscious," Bino said. "I've got to radio my dad and tell him what happened."

Bino grabbed the radio, but it fell apart into pieces. *Now what do we do, Christina thought.*

THE LION'S DEN

"Okay, it's time to go," Grant said, brushing dust and rock particles from his jeans. "We've got to move before they come for us!"

"I thought we wanted to be rescued," Mandisa observed. "So, shouldn't we stay here?"

"No," Christina replied. "There could be another rock slide. We need to get to a safe area."

"There won't be any more rock slides!" Grant shouted. "Just listen to me and let's move!"

The three children scrambled out of the Land Rover and ran after Grant, who had spun around the back of the vehicle and stopped behind the first boulder that had fallen. He peered around the side of the boulder at the mountain above.

"What are you looking at?" Christina asked. "What's going on?"

"There won't be any more rock slides," Grant explained, "because I saw a man push that second boulder over a ledge at us!"

"There they are!" Mandisa cried, her finger shaking as she pointed behind them. Three men were heading their way.

"Come on," Bino said. "Follow me." He used the biggest boulder to shield them from the men's sight as he led them down an animal path hidden in the brush. They kept moving until Bino found a hollow in the mountain. The group stopped there to watch the men approach the Land Rover.

The three men began shouting at each other. Christina couldn't understand what they were saying. "Why are they arguing?" she asked Mandisa, who had her hand over her mouth and her eyes open wide.

"They are blaming each other for letting us get away and for hurting the boss," Mandisa said.

"The boss!" Grant said. "What boss?"

"It's got to be Baruti!" Christina said. "He's behind the animal thefts, and those threatening notes to Dr. Applegate. Now, he's trying to scare us!"

"Oh, my," Bino said, watching Baruti climb out of the Land Rover and shake his head. He lifted his arms in the air and shouted at his men.

"What's he saying?" Christina asked.

"He is telling them to find us," Mandisa said. "He does not think we could have gone far."

"Let us prove him wrong," Bino said, moving further down the animal path.

As they hiked further, the mountain crevice began to narrow. Grant noticed Bino with his head down. "Are you okay, Bino?" he asked.

Bino shook his head. "Not really," he replied. "I have known Baruti as far back as I can remember. He and my father started working at the park the same year and have been friends ever since."

The crevice abruptly ended in a cave with an opening about four feet wide. "Uh, oh!" Grant said. "What do we do now? There are bad guys behind us and a dead end in front of us!" Grant frantically searched the walls surrounding them, but they were too flat to climb.

"Maybe we'll have a way out," Bino said. "Sometimes these caves have other exits. We must go in there and try to find one."

He took a deep breath and turned to face the other three kids. "Christina, give me your hand," he ordered. "Grant, take Mandisa's hand and Christina's hand. Don't let go."

As they moved further into the cave, the small amount of outside light **diminished** until Grant couldn't see his sister in front of him.

"This is getting a little scary," Christina said. Grant gulped and held her hand tighter.

"It's okay, everyone," Bino said. "You might just see a few bats and maybe some spiders in here, that's all."

Grrrrr...
Grrrrr...

Suddenly, a low, soft growl came from behind them. Then another...but this time, the sound was in front of them.

"Or," Bino whispered, "Maybe a lion or two."

BRAVE OR FOOLISH

"Stop," Bino whispered, as he listened in the darkness. He heard steady breathing. "I think they are asleep. Or at least most of them are! But we cannot move because we might bump into one of them and wake them."

"Grant," Christina whispered. "Do you have that pocket flashlight with you that Mimi gave you for your birthday last month?"

"Yes," Grant whispered. "I never leave home without it." He dropped Mandisa's hand, reached into his pocket, and pulled out the flashlight.

He pushed the switch and a dim yellow light glowed between his fingers. He slowly held up the beam and scanned it around the cave.

Christina quickly covered her mouth to stifle a scream as she gazed upon one lion after another. They were in a lion's den with about a dozen pure white lions and cubs!

"So this is where Bukekayo lives," Bino whispered. He pointed at the floor as he inched further into the cave. "There's a way out over there. Watch your step."

Christina couldn't take her eyes off the fluffy white cubs. "They are so sweet!" she whispered to Mandisa.

"Yes, they're real sweet," Bino observed, "but their parents are not! Let's move!"

After tiptoeing past the lions and their cubs, they moved farther into the cave system until they could see a tiny beam of light that grew brighter as they approached it.

"AAAHHHHHHH!"

ROARRRRR!

Suddenly, they heard the men yelling and shouting. They had obviously discovered the lions. Grant could hear feet shuffling as the men ran from the cave. The children walked a few more feet and finally found a small exit large enough for them to squeeze through.

"You go first, Mandisa," Grant said. "Then Christina. I'll bring up the rear," he told Bino.

"Okay," Bino said, as he helped Christina squeeze through the opening. He quickly followed her.

GRRRRRRRR!!!!

Grant was about to crawl through the opening when he heard the low growl. He pointed his flashlight in the direction of the sound. A camel-colored lion with a scruffy mane of fur around its head stared back at him. Grant knew it was the same lion, with the same gray eyes, he had encountered before on the savannah.

"Brave or foolish! Do I know the difference," Grant whispered softly.

He stared the lion straight in the eyes. Grant slowly knelt down to face him. Never taking his eyes or the flashlight off of the lion, he slowly crawled backwards through the opening. Just before losing sight of the lion, Grant watched him yawn and lay down. In a stronger voice than he expected, he heard himself say, "Maybe I'll see you again some time."

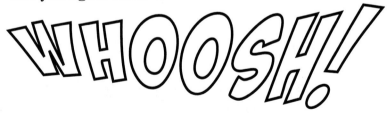

Suddenly, Grant was lifted and pulled out of the cave into the arms of the large black man who had been following them—at the airport, at the hotel, and at Dr. Applegate's office! He struggled to get free, swinging his head around wildly to find his sister.

"You look like you're okay, kid," the man said. Grant's eyes locked on a gold badge hanging on the man's belt. A policeman? This guy is a policeman? Grant was stunned.

Grant looked up to see Mimi running toward him with Papa, Dr. Applegate, Christina, Bino, and Mandisa close behind her. The inspector they had heard in Dr. Applegate's office was standing off to the side. Next to him were Baruti and his men, struggling to free themselves from the shiny, steel handcuffs around their wrists.

21

THAT'S
BRAVERY

Christina, Grant, Bino, and Mandisa sat on the porch of their luxury hut at the Hoyo Hoyo Tsonga Lodge.

"We sure had you wrong," Christina said to the inspector. "We thought you were the one stealing all the animals and threatening Dr. Applegate."

"He's been working with me," Dr. Applegate said. "I had contacted the authorities as soon as I realized some of our animals were missing.

I suspected that thieves were stealing them instead of them being killed by other animals, but I never suspected Baruti."

"How did you finally know it was him?" Grant asked.

"After the inspector searched my office," Dr. Applegate replied, looking at the inspector.

"I'm sorry," the inspector said. "My men made quite a mess."

"True," Dr. Applegate said, "but it was because of them and you four that I figured out it was Baruti."

"Us!" Christina exclaimed. "How?"

"Quite easily," Dr. Applegate replied. "When I got back to the office the next morning, I saw that the door to the office next to me was open. I knew Mandisa had been in the office, because there were lemon drops by the open window on the floor."

"Oops," Mandisa said. "I didn't know I had dropped any."

"Yes, well," Dr. Applegate said. "I had the office cleaned the day before, so I knew you were there that day. And your father said you were with Bino, Christina, and Grant that day, so I knew they were there too."

"I still don't see how you figured out it was Baruti," Grant said.

"My office floor was covered with files and paper everywhere," Dr. Applegate began. "But in the other office I found two pieces of paper. One was a receipt with my signature on it for selling a white lion. The other was Baruti's job application, which also had my signature on it."

"I hope you're not mad," Grant said. "I just grabbed it from the pile of papers to compare your signature from the receipt to it."

"No, no," Dr. Applegate said. "I compared the signature on the receipt to Baruti's signature. He did a pretty good job imitating my signature, but I noticed that the A's, T's, and R's matched his handwriting perfectly. That's when I knew Baruti was the thief. I contacted the inspector and we went to Baruti's farm, where we found all the animals caged up, including Bukekayo."

"After that," the inspector said, "we went after Baruti, found the Land Rover, and tracked him to the cave just as he and his men were being chased by the lions."

"That cave had lots of white lions in it," Bino said.

"I know," Dr. Applegate replied. "A few years back, your father and I found an abandoned tan-colored cub that had the recessive gene for producing white lions. Since then we've been breeding him and Bukekayo secretly. He lives in the den, but doesn't have the hunting instinct like the other lions. In fact, he's quite meek."

"Oh," Grant said, realizing that this must be the lion he had encountered.

"From what I understand," Dr. Applegate said, "you met him in the brush, Grant. He was probably trying to find Bukekayo. I'm surprised you didn't see him in the den."

"I did see him," Grant said, "just before leaving the cave. I thought I was so brave for staring down a **ferocious** lion, when he was really a tame lion."

"That doesn't matter one bit, Grant," Papa said. "You stared him down twice without panicking. That's what I call bravery!"

Mimi grabbed Grant and hugged him. "I think that's enough lion encounters for one safari," she said. "My heart is still thumping from your first face-to-face experience."

"RROOOAAARRR!"

Grant gave his best lion imitation and smiled. "Okay, Mimi! Maybe next time I'll stick to leopards!"

About the Author

Carole Marsh is an author and publisher who has written many works of fiction and non-fiction for young readers. She travels throughout the United States and around the world to research her books. In 1979 Carole Marsh was named Communicator of the Year for her corporate communications work with major national and international corporations.

Marsh is the founder and CEO of Gallopade International, established in 1979. Today, Gallopade International is widely recognized as a leading source of educational materials for every state and many countries. Marsh and Gallopade were recipients of the 2004 Teachers' Choice Award. Marsh has written more than 50 Carole Marsh Mysteries™. In 2007, she was named Georgia Author of the Year. Years ago, her children, Michele and Michael, were the original characters in her mystery books. Today, they continue the Carole Marsh Books tradition by working at Gallopade. By adding grandchildren Grant and Christina as new mystery characters, she has continued the tradition for a third generation.

Ms. Marsh welcomes correspondence from her readers. You can e-mail her at fanclub@gallopade.com, visit carolemarshmysteries.com, or write to her in care of Gallopade International, P.O. Box 2779, Peachtree City, Georgia, 30269 USA.

Built-In Book Club

Talk About It!

1. It's important to bring the necessary equipment when you go on a safari. If you were going on a safari, what would you bring?

2. What was your favorite part of the story? Why?

3. The children get to go camping during their safari. Have you ever been camping before? If so, what is your favorite thing about camping? If not, would you ever like to go camping with your family and friends?

4. While talking in their tent, the children encounter a snake. Have you ever had a close encounter with a snake in real life?

5. What is your favorite animal that lives in the African savanna? Why is it your favorite?

6. Were you frightened when Grant came face to face with the lion after he jumped out of the Land Rover? What should he have done instead? Why is it important to think about things before you do them?

7. Mandisa loves lemon drops and constantly shares them with her friends. What is your favorite type of candy?

8. If you could go on a safari, who would you like to bring along with you?

Built-In Book Club

Bring it to Life!

1. Draw it! Pretend you are on safari and you've forgotten your camera! Luckily, you have a piece of paper and drawing materials. Draw what you see on the African savanna. Make sure to include what animals you see. Can you see a watering hole? Is there a mountain or hills in the distance? Make your picture look as real as possible so you can show your friends and family when you get home.

2. Plan your own safari! Make a list of all the things you plan to bring along with you. What do you hope to see on your trip? How

many days will you be gone? Don't forget
to include who will be taking the adventure
with you!

3. How's the weather? Ask an adult to help
you use the Internet to learn about the weather
in South Africa during this time of year. Is it
hot and humid or cold and rainy? Compare the
weather in South Africa to the weather where
you live. Which do you like better? Why?

4. Display the colors! Find a picture of the
South African flag and draw a picture of it!
What is South Africa's national anthem? About
how many people live there? Find three other
interesting facts about South Africa and share
them with the members of your book club!

FASCINATING FACTS

about Africa, African Animals, and Kruger National Park

1. Kruger National Park was founded by Paul Kruger in 1898 and was originally called the Sabie Game Reserve.

2. The puff adder is a venomous viper species that can grow to over six feet long. The puff adder is responsible for more deaths than any other African snake.

3. The lion is the second largest cat on the planet with some males weighing over 550 pounds!

4. Johannesburg is home to more than three million people, making it the largest city in South Africa.

5. Today, Kruger National Park is connected to the Limpopo National Park in Mozambique and the Gonarezhou National Park in Zimbabwe, two of South Africa's neighboring countries.

6. Vervet monkeys have cheek pockets for storing food and have blue skin on their stomachs! Europeans exploring Africa commonly took vervet monkeys as pets.

7. Visitors to Kruger National Park are warned not to leave food lying about because monkeys and baboons will often steal it.

8. When a hippopotamus submerges in water, special muscles keep water from entering its nostrils and ears.

Glossary

amenity: something that provides comfort or pleasure

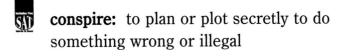 **conspire:** to plan or plot secretly to do something wrong or illegal

dehydrate: to lose water or moisture

delectable: greatly pleasing to taste, delightful

diminished: made to seem smaller or less, decreased

emit: to give off or send out, to give out a sound

ferocious: savage, extreme, or intense

fiendish: cruel, wicked, extremely bad

Glossary

inquisitive: liking to investigate, curious

mesmerized: to have your attention completely focused on something, to be fascinated

ravine: a deep depression in the land cut by a stream, with steep sides; smaller than a valley and larger than a gully

Visit the <u>carolemarshmysteries.com</u> website to:

- Join the Carole Marsh Mysteries™ Fan Club!

- Write a letter to Christina, Grant, Mimi, or Papa!

- Cast your vote for where the next mystery should take place!

- Find fascinating facts about the countries where the mysteries take place!

- Track your reading on an international map!

- Take the Fact or Fiction online quiz!

- Find out where the *Mystery Girl* is flying next!